Grandmother's
PEARLS

BJ CARLSON

ISBN 979-8-88685-972-0 (hardcover)
ISBN 979-8-88685-970-6 (digital)

Christian Faith Publishing
832 Park Avenue
Meadville, PA 16335
www.christianfaithpublishing.com

Printed in the United States of America

In honor of my sweet father-in-law, David Wesley Carlson, with love and thanks for being more like a father to me, showing Gods patience, love and grace in your daily walk.

Yet the Lord longs to be gracious to you; therefore He will rise up to show you compassion. For the Lord is a God of justice. Blessed are all who wait for Him!

—Isaiah 30:18 NIV

atie was so excited as she ran along the sidewalk. With her long brown hair flying straight behind her, she rounded the corner and flew up the steps to the massive front porch where her mother and father sat rocking and talking.

Her father was trying to decide the perfect time to present his lovely young daughter with the beautiful heirloom set of Hanadama Akoya pearls that his mother had passed down to him. He wanted her to have the genuine, polished, precious stones of beauty in time to wear on her wedding day, which was quickly approaching.

Katie couldn't believe in just a few short weeks, she would be married and living in her own home: no more jogging down the street every morning, stopping to give Mrs. Neal's dog, Beeswax, a treat, and no more waving to old Mr. Rutledge who used to teach her Sunday school class or Mrs. Linton who taught her high school English. So many changes were coming her way—some good and some sad. It made her think about her grandmother, Sara, her father's mother.

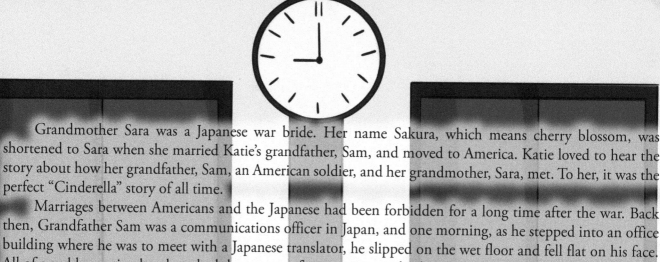

Grandmother Sara was a Japanese war bride. Her name Sakura, which means cherry blossom, was shortened to Sara when she married Katie's grandfather, Sam, and moved to America. Katie loved to hear the story about how her grandfather, Sam, an American soldier, and her grandmother, Sara, met. To her, it was the perfect "Cinderella" story of all time.

Marriages between Americans and the Japanese had been forbidden for a long time after the war. Back then, Grandfather Sam was a communications officer in Japan, and one morning, as he stepped into an office building where he was to meet with a Japanese translator, he slipped on the wet floor and fell flat on his face. All of a sudden, a tiny hand reached down as a soft sweet voice in broken English asked him, "You are okay?" As he lifted his face from the floor, he met the gaze of the most beautiful eyes he had ever seen. The sweet voice belonged to a small beautiful young woman, Sakura Keiko Shirasaki. As his hand touched hers, he knew he wanted to love and take care of her for the rest of their lives.

The marriage was very difficult to arrange and the paperwork daunting and exhaustive, but Grandfather Sam and Grandmother Sara were determined and committed to seeing it through. They were finally married in 1953, only seven months after they met. Both not only knew the perils and risks of prejudice and discrimination they would face in America but also knew they were meant for each other and were intent on making their relationship work.

Grandmother Sara told the enthralling story of her wedding day. Her father, unlike many of the other Japanese men, was so elated that his beautiful young daughter had found great happiness in a man that he knew would love and treasure her forever yet saddened at the thought that he might never again look into those deep, delightful, yet delicate eyes that were filled with excitement, adventure, and dreams in a world that he hoped would treat her kindly.

The day of her wedding, before giving her in marriage, Grandmother Sara's father drew out of his pocket a long thin box and gently laid it in her hands telling her, "The gift of the Hanadama Akoya pearls is so you can always remember where you're from but also because the Hanadama Akoya pearls, like you, are strong, beautiful, and carefully hand chosen and wonderfully knit together. They have the same shimmer I see in your beautiful eyes. I will always love you, Sakura, my darling!"

Katie never tired of hearing this fairytale story and was always dreaming of her wedding day, hoping she might also wear beautiful pearls and hear such adoring and captivating words.

As he watched Katie bounce up the steps, her dad thought about how much she reminded him of his mother. She had the same shiny dark-brown hair and small oval face that almost seemed too tiny for the large ebony eyes that always seemed to sparkle with a tiny hint of mischief and excitement.

Katie's father knew she had been eyeing a cheap set of imitation pearls downtown in the department store, and he hoped his gift would be in time to thwart her plans of spending her meager savings on imitation orbs of plastic. He thought about how the Hanadama Akoya pearls are a Japanese heritage and are far more expensive and more rare than the normal freshwater pearl. He had learned from his mother that they are a saltwater, cultured pearl from the Akoya oyster, and since the luster and size of each individual, unique pearl vary, diligent care and great effort are taken to hand sort and design a near-perfect arrangement of the most iridescent, almost mirrorlike finished pearls for each strand. The pearls are purposely and meticulously hand strung on strong silk cord and carefully knotted to hold each one in place. They are the strongest and most brilliant of all pearls. He smiled thinking how delighted Katie would be to wear his mother's timeless, finely detailed ornaments of beauty that she had been hoping for since she first heard her grandmother's tale of romance.

The beautiful blue October sky and gentle breeze were the perfect backdrop for the exciting news Katie had. She was out of breath, and tiny beads of sweat danced upon her temples with every beat of her racing heart as she pulled back her hair for her parents to see the dainty necklace hanging around her tiny neck. "I did it! I bought the beautiful pearls I've been admiring and saving for so I can wear them on my wedding day. Aren't they gorgeous?" She asked as she leaned in close for her parents to see.

Katie was so happy that even though these weren't the expensive, delightful pearls like her grandmother's, still, she could walk down the aisle wearing these gorgeous facsimiles upon her small round neck with her hair fixed up the same way as the beautiful wedding portrait of Grandmother Sara that was hanging in the den.

8

Oh my! thought Mother. "Oh no!" said Father quietly as the color drained from his face. What could he say at this point?

Katie was completely overjoyed with her great accomplishment. She skipped and danced about as she lovingly caressed the garland of tiny beads. She ran inside and bolted up the stairs so she could admire her wonderful purchase in the antique, floor-length mirror in her bedroom.

Katie swirled and curtsied as she pulled her hair up away from her face so she could get a better look at the cherished beads she had been envisioning upon her neck for months. She couldn't believe it. She had done it. She had saved her hard-earned money and single-handedly made one of her greatest dreams become reality.

As she went indoors to start supper, Katie's mother patted Father's shoulder and calmly told him everything would work out. Father prayed it would be so. What could he do now? He would never want to force his daughter to do or not do something. His love for her was too great for that. He would never want to destroy her hopes and joy or crush her dreams, but he wanted the best for her.

He knew the fake pearls wouldn't truly make her happy in the end, not when he had the genuine, original heirloom to give to her. How could he give this amazing gift to her now that she had found her own likeness to the beautiful inheritance he had arranged? She would never wholeheartedly love and treasure his gift as long as she had the self-gratification of obtaining her own. He knew he would have to be patient and lovingly and gently persuade her.

13

Katie dominated the table conversation at supper as she was getting more and more excited about her approaching wedding day. Her dress had been purchased six months before. Her mother's parents, Grandmother Rosie, and Poppy had brought back a lovely lace veil from their vacation in France. It had been cleaned and was hanging with the dress up in the attic…all ready for the big day. The bridesmaids had undergone the final fitting in their dresses, and the last bridal shower was given the evening before. All the flowers were ready and everything on the list completed. Now, the momentous countdown had begun. Everything was becoming very real.

Katie was an only child, and she knew it would be hard for her parents to let her go, but thankfully, she would only be a few miles away, unlike Grandmother Sara and her family.

As Katie was winding down from her meandering animated flow of chatter, Father asked if she would possibly think about returning the new beads she had purchased and wait for something more exquisite and charming. "You realize those aren't made very well and won't last very long, don't you, sweetheart?" He asked. Tears filled her large dark eyes as she placed her hand upon the cherished strand and ran from the table and up the stairs into her bedroom.

Katie lay across her bed burying her teary face into Mr. Tickles, her dear old teddy bear. He was threadbare in places, and one missing eye had been replaced by a button years ago. His stuffing had settled mostly into his belly. He was still a comfort to her as she remembered the day she received him for her third birthday and how she had named him because her father would tickle her as he gently shook him in her face.

Mr. Tickles had seen her through a lot of good and fun times, as well as bad and sad. No matter what secrets she told him, he always sat with the same look on his face, except for when she was eight years old and had used yellow thread to sew on his new button eye and add a few extra stitches on each side of his mouth to make a larger smile.

Katie still felt the same snugly consolation as she did when she would burrow into him on dark stormy nights when she was young or when she would hold him tight in tears from just breaking up with a boyfriend in her teen years.

"How could Father ask such a thing, Mr. Tickles? He knows I've been adoring these beads and saving every penny, waiting for the day I could make them mine." Oh, how her heart ached as she pondered what her father had said. Usually, she and Father got along really well. She always felt like she could tell him anything and he would understand. They could always talk things through. Father had always prayed with her about everything in her life. He had taught her the importance of pleasing God and having a relationship centered around faith in Jesus and growing in truth. Now, she was troubled and uncertain. She had truly thought Mother and Father would be delighted that she had saved her money and made a dream come true.

The days passed quickly. Each day, Father, in some way, confronted Katie about the necklace. Each day, she would grow more perplexed and troubled. She knew that this obviously was a very important matter if her father was bringing it up every day, but what was wrong with her wanting to do her own thing? After all, isn't that a part of growing and maturing, being responsible for yourself and making your own decisions?

Katie didn't want to start her new married life having a conflict with Father, but she loved her pearls and wasn't ready to give them up. Certainly, Father could appreciate that. Every day, she could see a deep sadness in his eyes. She wished they had time to sit down together and talk, but things with the wedding were moving too fast, and she just didn't have time to slow down. *Maybe*, she thought, *after the wedding and honeymoon and things settle down, we can get together and have one of our long talks like we used to.*

Katie's wedding day finally arrived. Her father had taken her floor-length mirror, dress, and all her wedding day preparations over to the large new dressing room at their church. The smell of her favorite breakfast, pancakes and bacon, with little flower strawberries and maple syrup wafted up the stairs as Katie lay in bed thinking about the day's events. She was so excited! By the end of the day, she would be Mrs. Alexander James Monroe, and they would be flying to Puerto Rico to board a ten-day Caribbean cruise.

Everything during the past few months had seemed like a blur, yet Katie still had a sad feeling in her heart about her father. She would just have to put it out of her mind for now and enjoy the "treatment like a queen" morning her mother had planned for her.

19

Katie had her breakfast in bed as she watched the sunrise from her bedroom window. It was a cool morning with a little frost. The strawberries cut into little flowers made Katie smile. Her mother had always tried to make meals not only delicious but also fun and appealing. The pancakes and bacon were yummy and filling, which was good because with all the preparation for the wedding, she probably wouldn't eat again until the afternoon wedding-reception tea, which wouldn't be until around 2:00 p.m.

Such a rush of emotions was going through Katie's mind as she thought what it would be like to not wake up in her bed anymore, to not sit at the breakfast table with her parents, and to have all the responsibilities to handle for herself. She knew she could always depend on her parents if she really needed them, but they had taught her how to be a capable, confident adult. She knew she was ready, yet it was sad to leave the place she had always felt safe, secure, and nurtured.

When Katie arrived at the church, she was met by her best friends—Amy, Laurel, and Olivia—who swooped her up and whisked her away into the dressing room. What a fun time of laughing, joking, and sharing flashbacks of their almost twenty years of memories together as they dressed for one of the most important days of Katie's life.

Amy and Laurel had each lived on each side of Katie's house since they were all toddlers. They had grown up together more like sisters than friends. Their families were always having cookouts and parties, as well as vacationing together.

Olivia had moved into the house across the street when Katie was six and quickly became just as close to her as her other two friends. They were always borrowing each other's clothes and doing fun things together.

Olivia was also one year older than the rest of them and had been married for seven months, so she was fulfilling the duties of matron of honor. They giggled at how old that made her sound. Katie gave each of them a beautiful necklace with a tiny diamond and a small inscription badge with their name and the date and gave each a hug.

It was almost time. Katie trembled as she turned to look at herself in the mirror. Mother had been in to check on her earlier and told her how radiant she looked. She didn't stay long as she had already taken time to talk to Katie that morning when she brought breakfast up.

Katie's mother was a very beautiful and intelligent woman who always seemed to have the answer for anything and everything. She ran a very organized home, taught Bible study, and helped out down at the local homeless shelter, but she always had time to make Katie and her father feel like they were the most loved and cherished of all people.

Katie hoped she would be like her mother in many ways. She wanted to be a loving wife and mother and teach her children the importance of always putting God first. Katie's thoughts were cut short when the wedding planner came for the other girls and told her she had about ten minutes before her father would be in to get her.

As Katie stood in front of the mirror, carefully putting on the final touch, the beautiful necklace she had purchased, the clasp popped off, and all her beautiful pearls went tumbling all around her. She gasped in horror as tears filled her eyes. She quickly bent down, collecting every little beloved, broken one. The door opened, and her father came in just as she was turning to get up. He saw the sorrow in her eyes and the pain portrayed in her tender face as he reached to help her up. She burst into tears as she handed him her broken hopes and dreams.

"I'm so sorry I didn't listen to you, Father. I knew deep down that these wouldn't last. I was so excited. I wore them out trying them on over and over. You tried to tell me, but I wouldn't listen. I'm so sorry and sad that I didn't."

"It's okay!" Father told her. "Dry your tears, and let's get you freshened up. It's time to go meet your new husband."

Katie's father waited until she was ready to go, then reached into his pocket and pulled out a small timeworn box, and gently laid it in her hand. She couldn't breathe as she stared down at the lovely grouping of stunning pearls.

"Wer…were these Grandmother Sara's?" she asked. "The very same," replied Father. "I've wanted to give them to you for some time, but I had to wait until you were ready.

This gift of heirloom pearls is not only a gift of strength and beauty just like you, precious daughter, but also a reminder that we don't have to work so hard in life to arrange our own blessings, which ultimately crumble around us, or grasp for the fake treasures the world offers. When we wait for the true treasures and blessings that God has for each of us, we find they are much more lasting and fill us so much more deeply than our own temporary, imperfect achievements. I hope you cherish these as much as I will always love and cherish you, my dear Katie."

With that, he lovingly clasped them around Katie's small neck. As they stood staring into the mirror before them, Katie kissed her father's cheek and told him how thankful she was for his patience, wisdom, and unchanging love.

Notes from the Author

Just like the extraordinary pearls in this story, we are also carefully chosen and knit together for a special purpose. We are fearfully and wonderfully made. If we choose to have Jesus in our lives, He can make something beautiful and wonderful in us.

So often, we do everything in our own power to make our desires become reality, and as they each one fail and begin to crumble around us, we choose to grab ahold to every tiny broken little one instead of giving all our brokenness to the One who can replace them with genuine treasures to be cherished throughout eternity.

It is sad but true that not everyone has a loving, wise, and patient earthly father like the father in this story, but everyone can have a loving, wise, and patient Heavenly Father. If you don't belong to Christ, if God isn't your Heavenly Father, it is the author's prayer and hope that you might choose to give up your fake, earthly treasures that fall to pieces around you and exchange them for God's heavenly riches that are eternal, strong, and lasting.

Life won't always be perfect, but with God's grace and mercy in your life, you can know the special plans He has for you and make it through any difficulties that come your way, with a peace that you can never find in this world.

Scriptures to Meditate On

For you created my inmost being; you knit me together in my mother's womb. I praise you because I am fearfully and wonderfully made; your works are wonderful, I know that full well. My frame was not hidden from you when I was made in the secret place, when I was woven together in the depths of the earth. Your eyes saw my unformed body; all the days ordained for me were written in your book before one of them came to be. How precious to me are your thoughts, God! How vast is the sum of them! Were I to count them, they would outnumber the grains of sand. (Psalm 139:13–18a NIV)

For we are God's handiwork, created in Christ Jesus to do good works, which God prepared in advance for us to do. (Ephesians 2:10 NIV)

"For I know the plans I have for you," declares the Lord, "plans to prosper you and not to harm you, plans to give you hope and a future. Then you will call on me and come and pray to me, and I will listen to you. You will seek me and find me when you seek me with all your heart. I will be found by you," declares the Lord... (Jeremiah 29:11–14a NIV)

For all have sinned and fall short of the glory of God, and all are justified freely by his grace through the redemption that came by Christ Jesus. God presented Christ as a sacrifice of atonement, through the shedding of his blood—to be received by faith. (Romans 3:23–25a NIV)

If you declare with your mouth, "Jesus is Lord," and believe in your heart that God raised him from the dead, you will be saved. For it is with your heart that you believe and are justified, and it is with your mouth that you profess your faith and are saved. (Romans 10:9–10 NIV)

Would you like to make that choice right now by joining the author in this prayer?

Heavenly Father, I realize by reading these scriptures that I am wonderfully and fearfully made by Your hands for great things. I also accept the truth from these scriptures that I am a sinner, but through faith, I can be justified by trusting that Jesus gave atonement for my sins through His shed blood. I do believe these things I have read, and I accept Your grace and redemption through Jesus. I invite You to be the Lord of my life, and I thank you for this wonderful gift of salvation. Amen.

About the Author

BJ Carlson is a seasoned author who lives in the Midwest with her adorably sweet husband who is her best friend and personal slayer of dragons. They have three grown children and nine grandchildren. BJ loves to write stories and modern-day parables that will captivate and encourage not only her family, but also many others. Nothing brings her more joy than to hear laughter or see someone enjoying something she has created.

Throughout the years, moving with her husband, from place to place, while in the military, opened up many opportunities for BJ to use her writing and artistic skills in various ways. Although this is her first work to be published in many years, she has written poetry, short stories, plays, and Sunday school and Bible-study lessons that have been used in churches across the country. She grew up in the south and gave her life to Jesus at a very early age.

Like her Heavenly Father, she is a lover of souls. Her main goal and principle in life are expressed in a quote she penned many years ago: "Treat life and every person in light of eternity." She hopes to draw people—young and old—to her Savior, Jesus, through her art and writings.